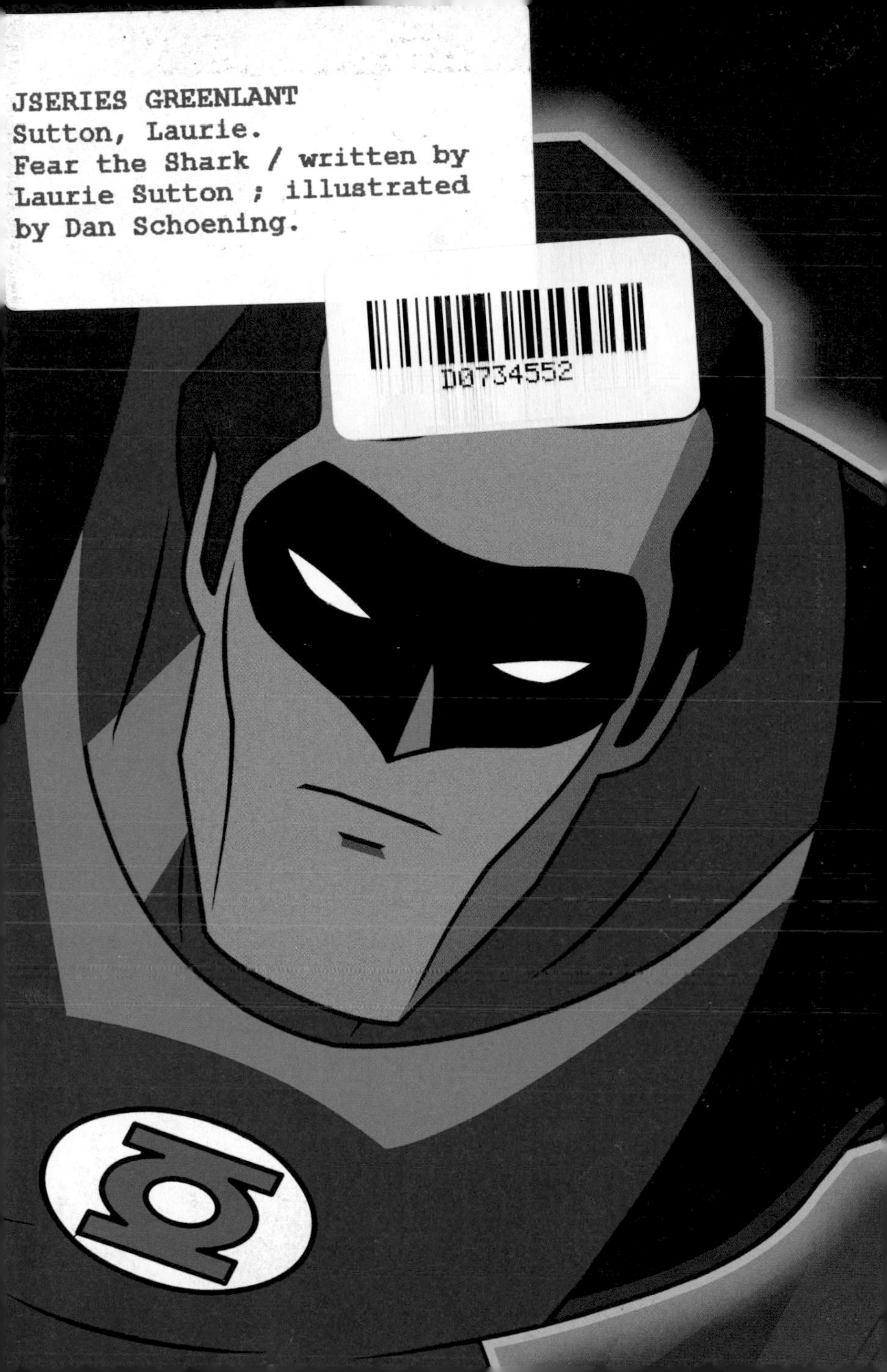

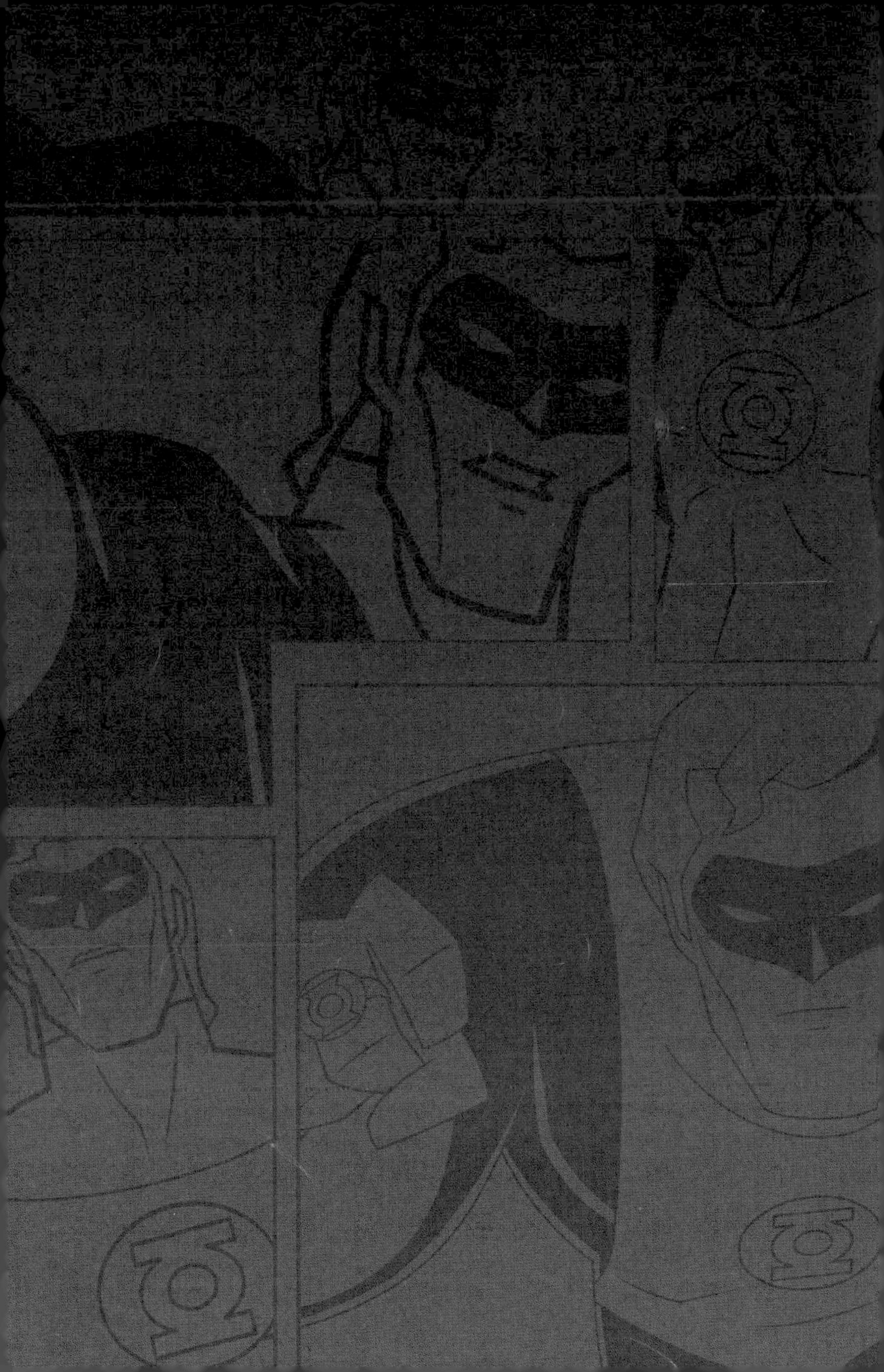

AS THE NEWEST MEMBER OF AN INTERGALACTIC PEACEKEEPING FORCE KNOWN AS THE GREEN LANTERN CORPS, HAL JORDAN FIGHTS EVIL AND PROUDLY WEARS THE UNIFORM AND RING OF . . .

SUPER DC HEROES

GREEN LANTERN

FEAR THE SHARK

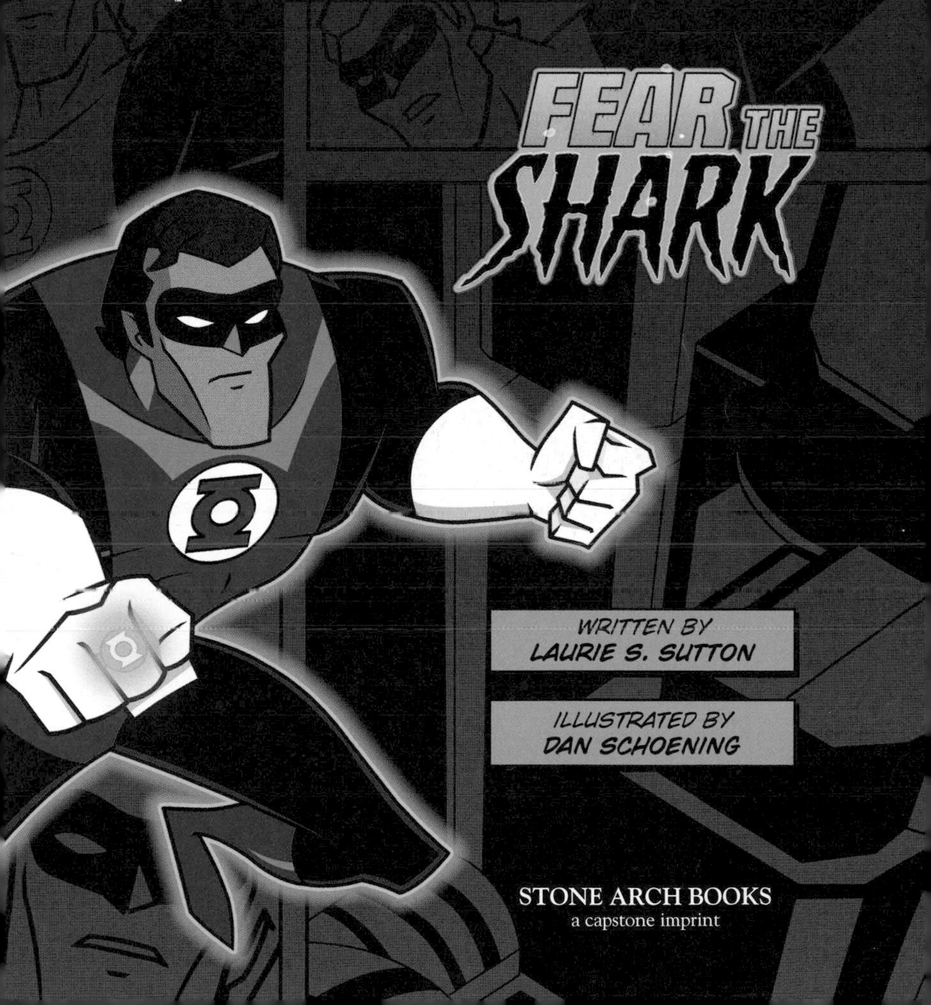

WRITTEN BY
LAURIE S. SUTTON

ILLUSTRATED BY
DAN SCHOENING

STONE ARCH BOOKS
a capstone imprint

Published by Stone Arch Books in 2012
A Capstone Imprint
151 Good Counsel Drive, P.O. Box 669
Mankato, Minnesota 56002
www.capstonepub.com

Library of Congress Cataloging-in-Publication Data
Sutton, Laurie.
  Fear the Shark / written by Laurie Sutton ; illustrated by Dan Schoening.
    p. cm. -- (DC super heroes)
  ISBN-13: 978-1-4342-2620-4 (library binding)
  ISBN-13: 978-1-4342-3406-3 (pbk.)
  1. Green Lantern (Fictitious character)--Juvenile fiction. 2. Superheroes--
Juvenile fiction. 3. Supervillains--Juvenile fiction. [1. Superheroes--Fiction. 2.
Supervillains--Fiction.] I. Schoening, Dan, ill. II. Title.
  PZ7.S968294Fe 2012
  813.54--dc22   2011005153

Summary: Something fishy is at work in Coast City. A new super-villain rises
from the peaceful waters — the Shark, who uses telepathy and oceanic powers
to feed off the citizens' frenzy and fright. Luckily, citizen Hal Jordan is secretly
the Green Lantern. His power ring should be able to liquidate the Shark's
weapons. But when the slippery predator sends a tsunami toward the city, can
the Emerald Crusader stop the mounting wave of fear?

Art Directors: Bob Lentz and Brann Garvey
Designer: Hilary Wacholz
Production Specialist: Michelle Biedscheid

Printed in the United States of America in Stevens Point, Wisconsin.
032011
006111WZF11

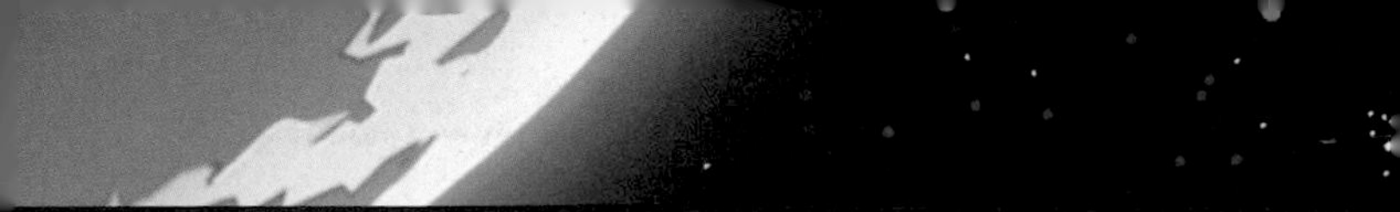

TABLE OF CONTENTS

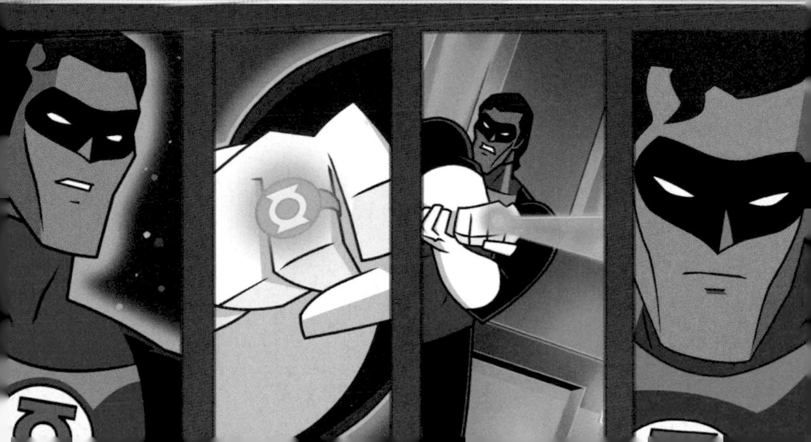

CHAPTER 1

SOMETHING FISHY

It was a perfect day for a walk in the park. The sun was shining, the birds were chirping, and Hal Jordan had the day off. He had just finished his patrol as the Green Lantern of Space Sector 2814. There were no planets in danger. No galactic disasters. The universe was peaceful . . . almost.

"Help!" a little girl screamed.

Hal Jordan tensed for danger. He was the Green Lantern of Earth and had sworn an oath to fight evil. Hal looked around for the menace to the girl.

"Robert! Don't scare your sister like that!" the girl's father said.

"Aw, Dad!" a young boy replied. "I was just playing."

Hal smiled. The threat was nothing more than a brother teasing his sister, a danger that happened all over the galaxy.

"Come on, you two," the dad said. "The fountain show is about to start."

The Coast City Park was putting on a special performance. New high-tech fountains had been built in the lake. They gushed and squirted water in time to classical music.

Today, there was an orchestra with a conductor to play the songs. A large crowd had gathered around the fountains, and Hal found a place to watch as well.

The show started with a dramatic clash of cymbals. A geyser burst up from the lake and then suddenly stopped. Sprinkles of water came down like snowflakes. At the same time, other smaller fountains gushed upward, twirled around in circles, and spiraled downward. The audience cheered.

WHOOOOSH!

Another giant pillar of water exploded from the lake. But this time the orchestra did not expect it, and their music stopped in the middle of a song. This effect was not part of the performance!

Hal Jordan didn't hesitate. Even if the danger was minor, he couldn't ignore it. He was a Green Lantern and would help in any situation.

Hal wore a special ring that had the power to create anything out of green energy. It was made by the Guardians of the Universe and was the most powerful weapon ever created. Now Hal would need it to stop a runaway water fountain.

Everyone in the crowd had their eyes on the gusher. No one noticed Hal Jordan use his ring to transform his regular clothes into his Green Lantern uniform.

He recited the sacred oath of the Green Lantern Corps:

"In brightest day,
In blackest night,
No evil shall escape my sight.
Let those who worship evil's might,
Beware my power —
Green Lantern's light!"

The super hero was ready for action!

First, Hal commanded his power ring to form a giant thumb. The green energy flowed out of the ring and took shape. Then he took the thumb and plugged the fountain with it.

SQUEAK! The water stopped.

"An easy fix," Green Lantern said.

Just then, the smaller fountains started gushing wildly. Water shot out toward the audience. **FWOOSHHHHHH!!**

The powerful streams knocked people off of their feet.

"Those fountains aren't programmed to do that!" Green Lantern said to himself. "How can this be happening?"

"The program has not malfunctioned," the power ring said in an electronic voice. "An outside cause is detected."

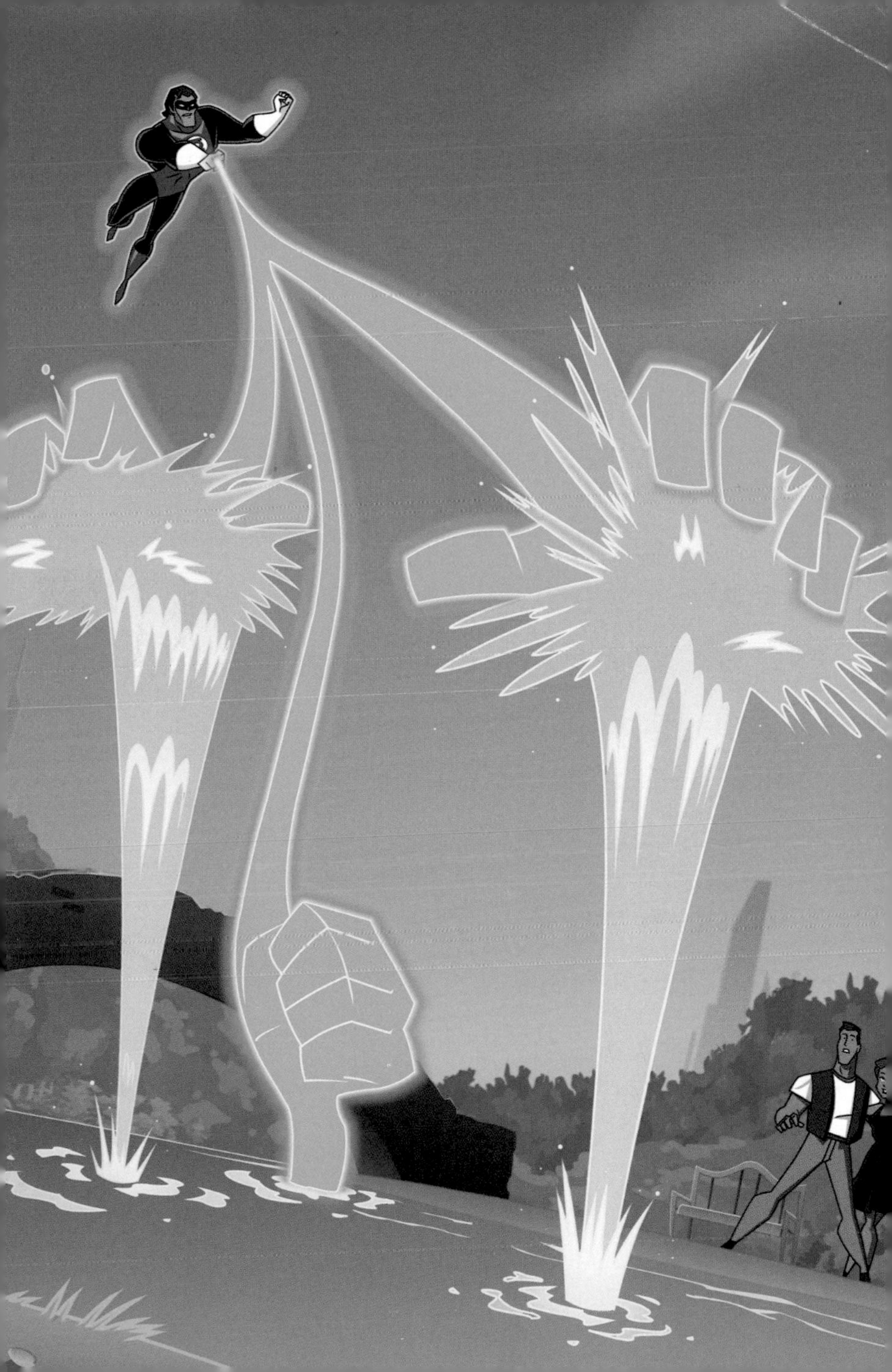

"I'd better stop this!" Green Lantern shouted. "People are getting hurt."

The mob scattered in every direction. Everyone was afraid. Fear was a bigger problem than the out-of-control gushers — even Green Lantern was feeling it.

"There's nothing to be afraid of," the hero told himself. "It's just water!"

As soon as Green Lantern set his mind on that thought, the fear drained out of him. He flew into the air above the lake. He aimed the power ring at the shooting fountains. BARROOOOOMM!!

A stream of green energy swirled around the spouting water. Then Green Lantern commanded it to take the shape of puppies and kittens. Suddenly, the gushers turned into playful animals.

"Ooooh!" a little girl said with a laugh. "Look at the kitties!"

"That looks like my dog!" a boy said.

The crowd stopped running away. Instead, they watched the green animals bounce in the air. Green Lantern made the critters chase each other around in circles, and the audience applauded. They thought the effects were part of the show.

Green Lantern hovered above the lake. He saw a dark shape moving in the water below. He didn't know what it was, but the evil creature was probably the cause of the trouble.

ZZZAPPPPPPP! Green Lantern used his ring to form a giant green fishing net. He scooped up the dark shape with the net and pulled it out of the lake.

"The Shark!" Green Lantern exclaimed.

Inside the net was a man with a shark's head. The villain gasped for breath in the dry air.

"Green Lantern!" the Shark said. "Long time, no *sea*!"

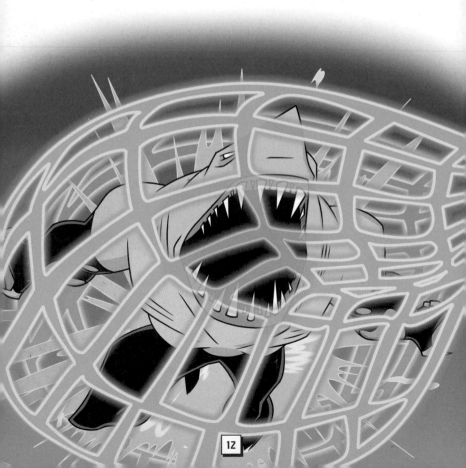

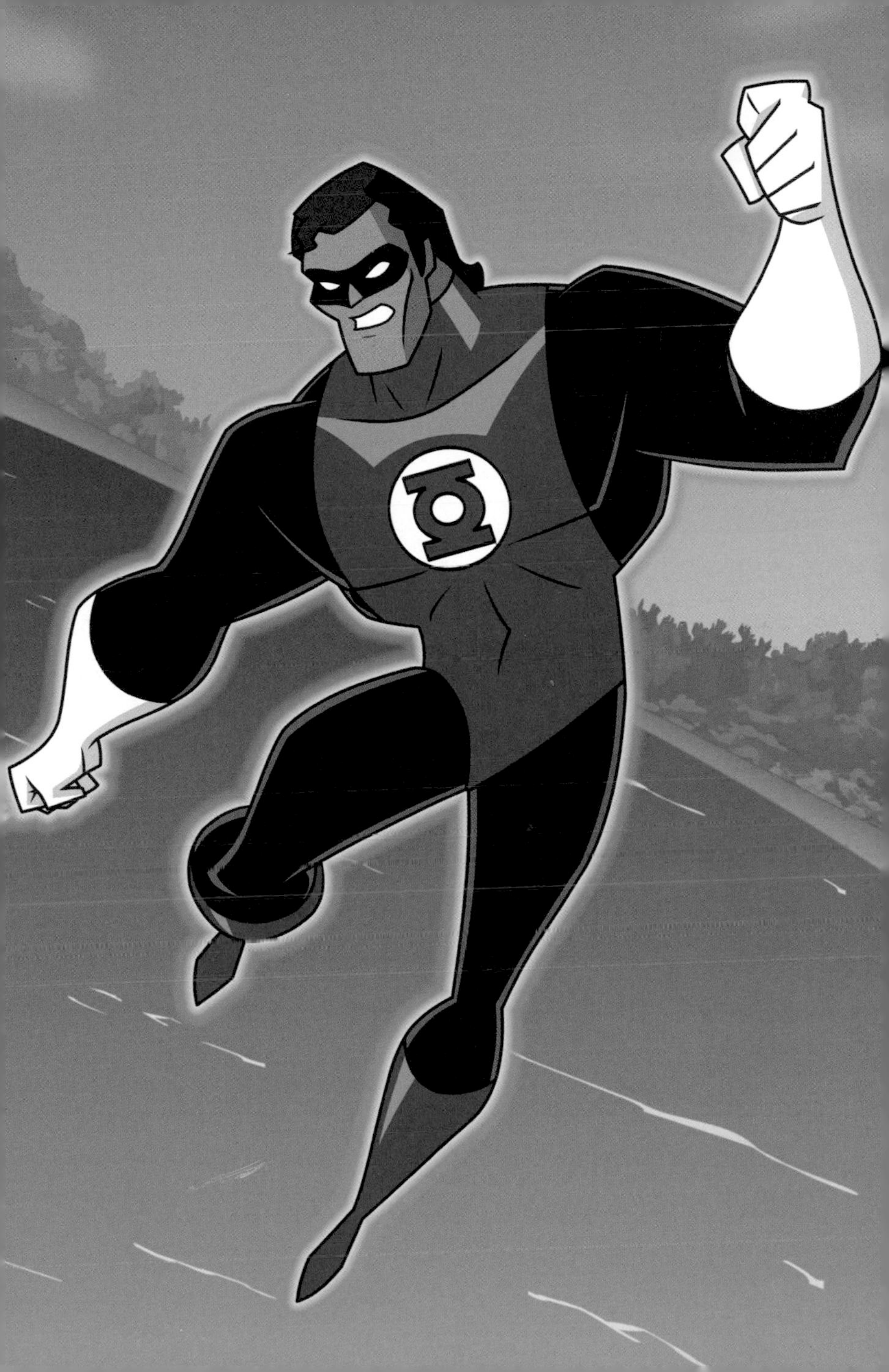

CHAPTER 2

THE TASTE OF FEAR

Green Lantern hadn't seen the Shark in years. The underwater marauder, with a human body and a shark's head, had been an ordinary shark once. Then one day, radiation from nuclear waste mutated him into this evolved form. The Shark was half human, but he still had all the instincts of the greatest predator in the sea. He also had very sharp teeth.

CRUNCH! The Shark chomped down on the net Green Lantern had created. The energy strands snapped like noodles.

SPLASH! The Shark dropped back into the lake. Green Lantern followed. The hero used his ring to create scuba gear to go under water and soon came face to face with his old enemy again.

"Shark!" Green Lantern said. "So you're behind the fountains going crazy."

"That trick wasn't hard to do with my powerful mind," the Shark bragged.

"I've defeated you so many times. Why did you come back?" Green Lantern asked.

"Because humans fear me. I was born a tiger shark. Tiger! Shark! Those two words terrify people," the villain explained. "Their fear is food for me."

"So you came to Coast City for a little snack?" Green Lantern said. "My hometown isn't a buffet."

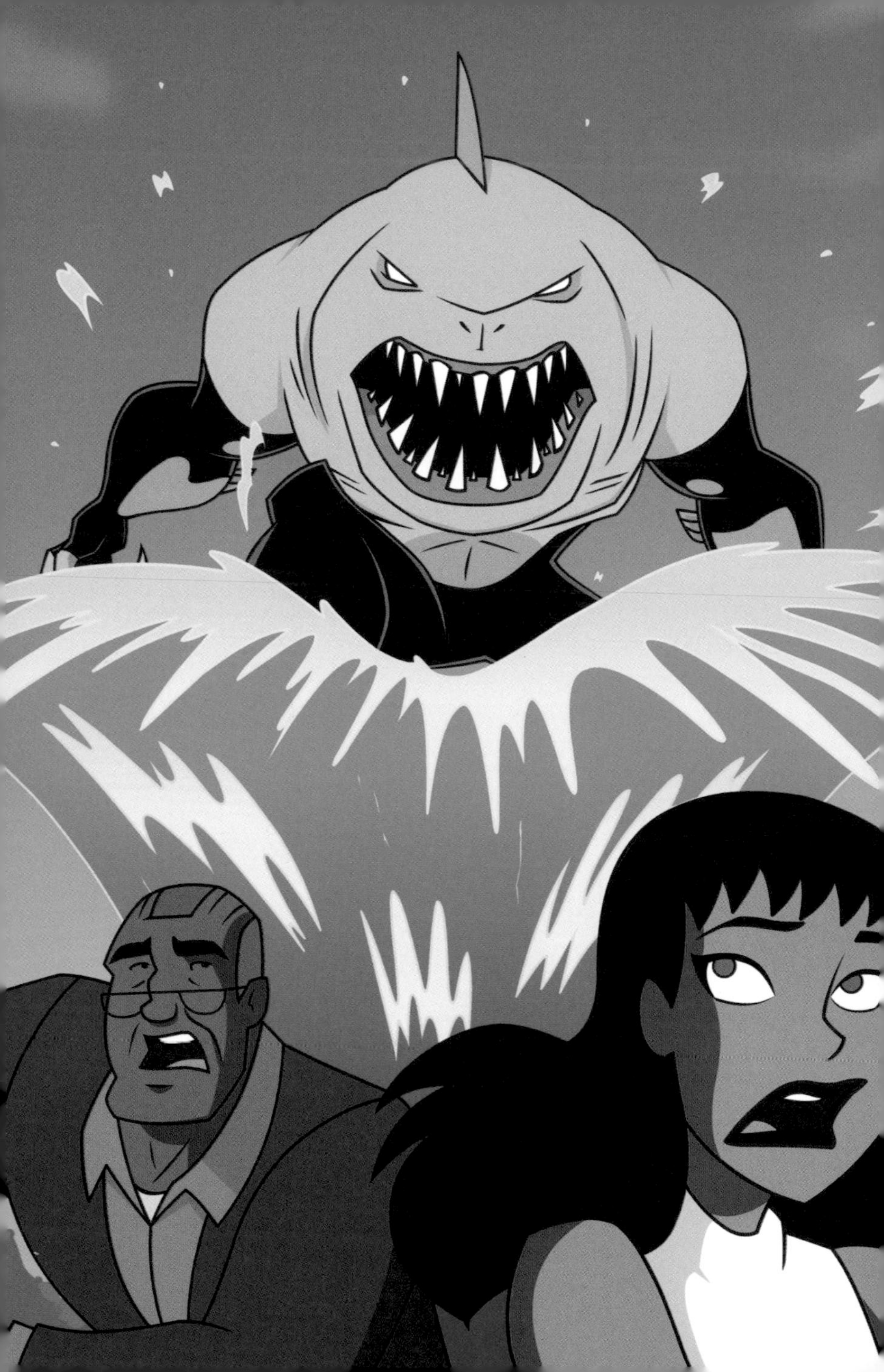

"No, it's a banquet!" the Shark said, laughing. His wide mouth exposed rows and rows of razor-sharp teeth.

The Shark swam to the surface of the lake. He used his mind to create a giant pedestal of water to stand on. As soon as people saw him, they began to scream and run away. The Shark absorbed their fear. He fed on it like a hungry animal.

"Mmmm! Tasty!" he said.

Green Lantern flew up out of the lake. He saw the crowd running around in panic because of the Shark. Green Lantern commanded his power ring to form fluffy pillows everywhere.

POOF! POOF!

The people bumped into them safely instead of crashing into each other.

Everyone laughed and bounced around on the green pillows. Their fear was gone.

"Grrrr, Green Lantern!" the Shark growled. "Now I have to find another feeding ground."

SPLASH! The Shark jumped back into the lake, but Green Lantern was right behind him. The villain swam straight for a big pipe, which was used to pump water out of the lake in case of an emergency. He darted inside, and Green Lantern followed.

It was dark inside the pipe. It was a tight fit, too. Green Lantern should have been afraid of getting stuck or not being able to see. He wasn't. This was nothing compared to battling space monsters or fighting superpowered aliens. The Shark wouldn't get a morsel of fear out of him.

Green Lantern chased the Shark through the city's water supply system. It was a maze filled with water. The pipes led them left and right, up and down. After a while there was no way to tell where they were. Now it was the Shark's turn to feel dread. How was he going to get out?

WHAM! A glowing green cage slammed shut around the Shark. The villain was caught! His own fear had distracted him from his pursuer.

"You're a slippery one," Green Lantern said, "but I've got you now!"

"You'll never find your way out of here, either!" the Shark said, still trying to frighten his enemy.

"No problem," Green Lantern replied. "Ring, locate the nearest exit."

A three-dimensional map formed in the water in front of Green Lantern, showing the maze of pipes. A small green lantern symbol appeared in the center of the maze. At the top of the map was a blinking X. A dotted line connected them.

"See? Not to worry," Green Lantern said. "The ring will show me the way."

Green Lantern dragged the angry Shark in his cage through the city water system toward the exit. Soon they were floating below a manhole cover. Light came down through the slots in the heavy metal disk.

"There's the light at the end of the tunnel," Green Lantern said. "And it's the end of the line for you, Shark."

"I still have some fight left in me," the Shark said.

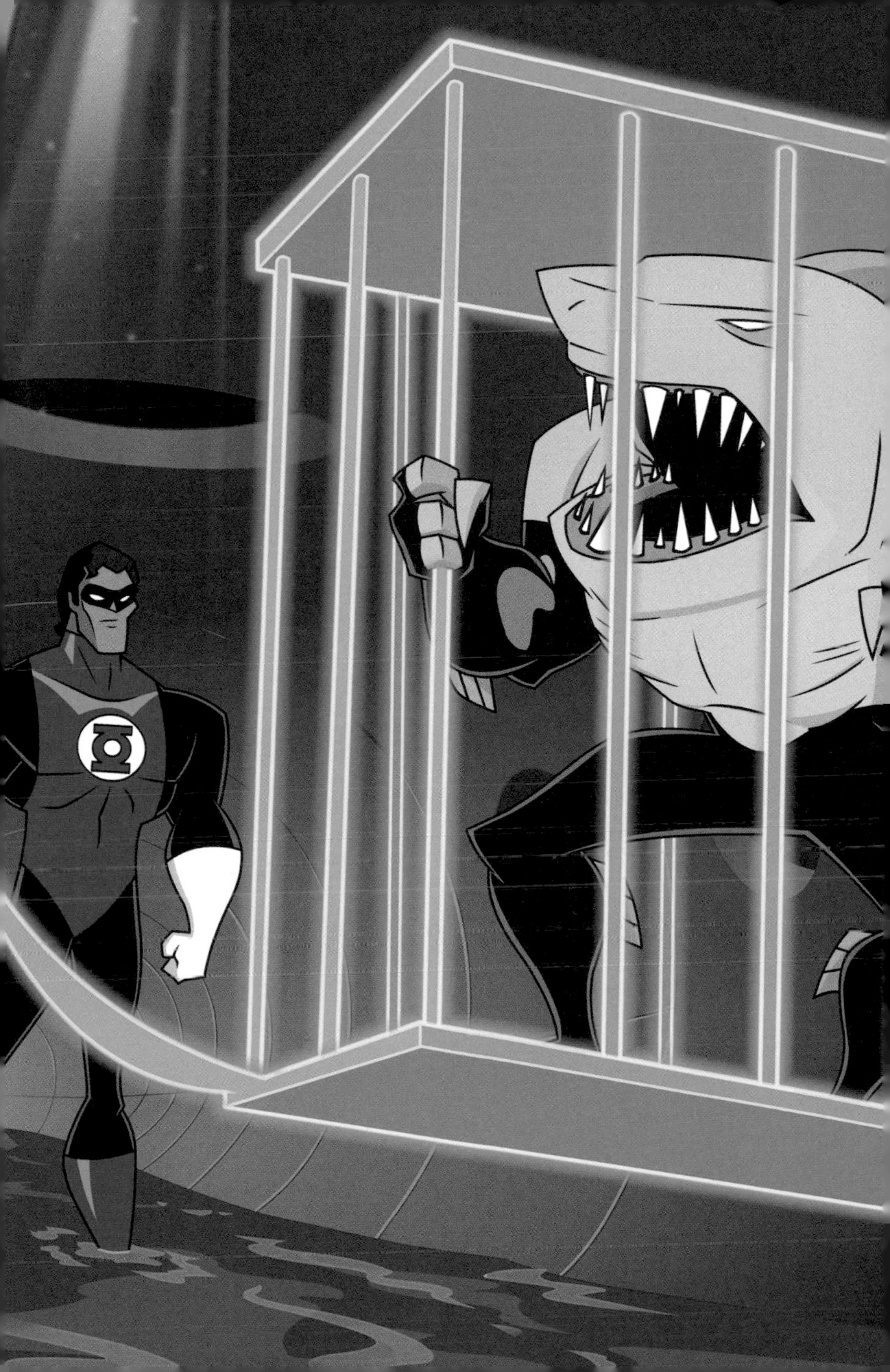

WHOOOOSH!

A gush of water threw Green Lantern up toward the manhole cover.

WHAM! He smashed into the thick iron plate. Green Lantern was stunned and lost his hold on the green energy cage. The Shark broke free! He swam up the column of water he had created and through the open manhole.

Cars skidded. Tires squealed. The manhole was in the center of a busy street, and the Shark was in the middle of rush-hour traffic!

CHAPTER 3

WATER FIGHT

"Get out of the way! Are you crazy?" the driver of a minivan yelled.

SMASH! The Shark slammed his fists on the hood of the vehicle, and the metal dented. Then he crawled up to the windshield and bared his teeth at the man.

"Ah!" the man shrieked.

The Shark grabbed the driver by the collar of his shirt. "Where do you think you're going, tidbit?" the Shark said. "Your fear feeds me."

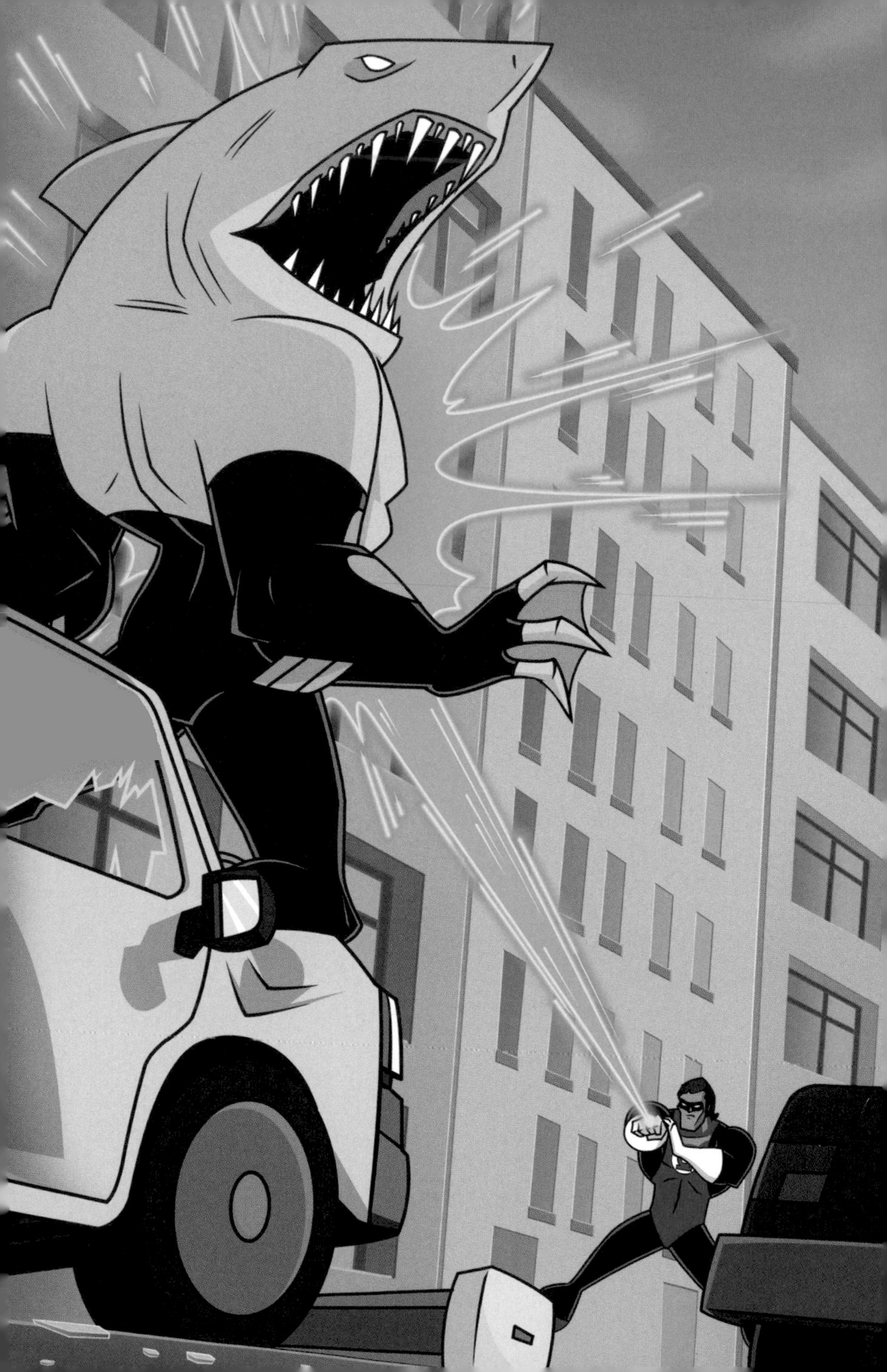

A giant green fist slammed into the Shark. The villain was knocked away from the helpless man. Green Lantern flew up out of the manhole and toward the Shark. His power ring crackled with energy.

The Shark made a nearby fire hydrant pop its top. Water spewed out. Then another hydrant down the street did the same thing. Then another and another.

Soon, the whole block was flooded with water. The street was like a river. All the cars started floating away, and the people inside them cried for help.

"All this fear is like a feast!" the Shark said.

Green Lantern flew above the flooded street. He used the power ring to create a gigantic ferryboat. Then he lifted each vehicle onto the ferry with big green tongs. Soon, everyone was out of the water and safe on the boat.

Next, Green Lantern had to plug the powerful hydrants. He commanded the ring to form a super-size pair of pliers. He used them to pinch the hydrants shut one by one, and the water stopped gushing at last.

WHOOOOSH! A colossal wave rose up in the middle of the street. The Shark rode on the top of it.

"I'm still hungry!" the villain said. "I need more fear to feed me."

The wave began to move. It headed right for Green Lantern's ferryboat.

The people saw the churning water coming at them. Then they looked up and saw Green Lantern in the sky.

"Green Lantern will protect us!" a man shouted. "There's no reason to be afraid!"

"Yeah! That crazy shark guy can't hurt us," a little girl said.

The Shark felt the crowd's fear fade. Their worry got smaller and smaller until there wasn't even a speck. The villain had nothing left to feed his hunger.

"I need a new menu," the Shark said, using his mind powers to direct the wave of water away from the ferryboat. He rode on top of it like a surfer.

The wave rolled down the street and took all the water with it. As soon as it had passed by, the pavement was dry.

Green Lantern dissolved the green ferry so that the cars could drive on the road again. Then he went after the Shark.

The super-villain was not hard to find. Who else would be riding a giant wave in the middle of Coast City? Green Lantern caught up with the Shark in no time.

"It's time for you to leave this restaurant," Green Lantern said.

"The food is great, but the service is terrible," the Shark replied.

His wave was heading toward a marina. Boats of all sizes were tied up at the docks. There were many people on the boats enjoying the beautiful day.

Green Lantern saw where the Shark was going. The wave would swamp the boats at the marina and then sink them.

Green Lantern commanded his ring to create a dam between the harbor and the Shark's wave. The wave slammed into the green wall and burst like a water balloon.

Splash! Nothing was left of it except for a few puddles on the ground.

"Hey, where'd the Shark go?" Green Lantern wondered aloud. The villain was nowhere in sight.

"Oh no!" someone screamed.

Green Lantern looked toward the sound, which came from the harbor. A tremendous whirlpool was forming in the water.

"There he is," Green Lantern said. "Up to his old tricks."

The Shark stood in the center of the swirling water. He was using his mind to create the disaster.

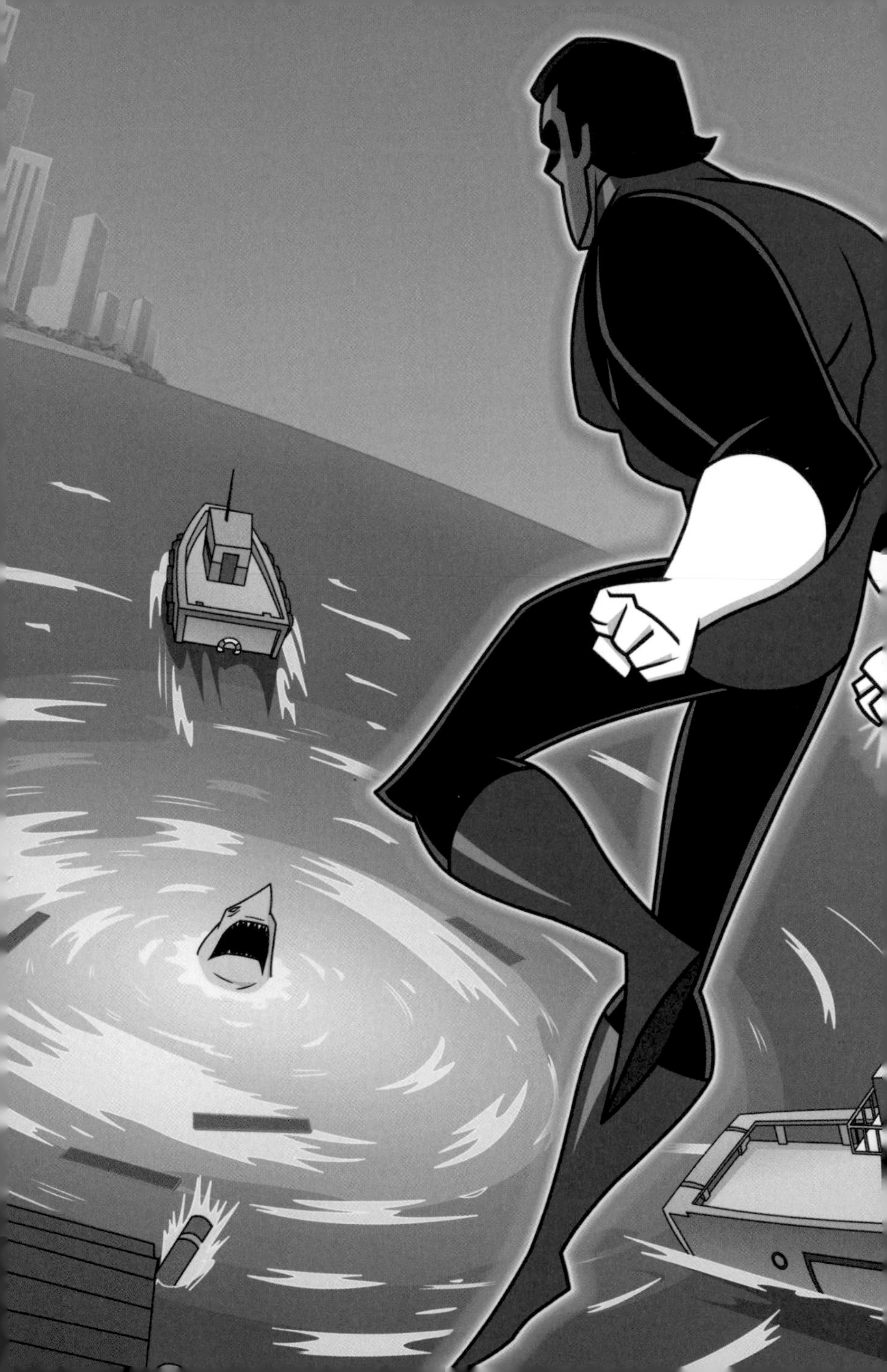

Boats were getting sucked into the whirlpool. Some tipped over and spilled people into the water. Hundreds of onlookers were terrified.

"Feed me! Feed me!" the Shark said as he absorbed their fear.

The Shark was too busy feeding to notice Green Lantern creating green dolphins and turtles and manatees with his power ring. The sea creatures swam all over the harbor and rescued the people in the water. Soon everyone was safe.

Then Green Lantern created a giant green paddle. He used it to stir against the spin of the whirlpool and stop the vortex. Finally, the danger was gone, but so was the Shark.

CHAPTER 4

SHARK BAIT

Green Lantern patrolled the waters along the shores of Coast City looking for the Shark. He knew his enemy could not be far away. The Shark was not finished making trouble.

Green Lantern used his power ring to form a mini-sub so he could search for the Shark in the deep water. He also created an army of undersea creatures to help him. Dolphins, whales, and jellyfish searched the kelp forests and the coral reefs for the Shark. No one could find him.

At last, a little green octopus swam up to the sub. It waved all eight arms at Green Lantern to get his attention. Then it pointed one of its tentacles at something in the distance. The octopus squirted away in that direction, and Green Lantern followed in the sub.

Soon, the super hero saw an old shipwreck. "That would make a good hiding place for the Shark," he said.

The octopus swam inside the wreck. Green Lantern changed the mini-sub into scuba gear so he could fit inside the sunken ship. He followed the little octopus to a passenger cabin. The eight-limbed creature pointed at something inside.

The Shark!

The underwater villain was not moving.

The Shark was stretched out on a bed covered in seaweed. His eyes were closed, and bubbles rose from his gills. Then Green Lantern heard a snore. He was sleeping!

"The Shark's taking a siesta after his big meal," Green Lantern said to himself. "Well, nap time is over."

Green Lantern swam into the cabin. Even asleep, the Shark sensed the change in water pressure. Suddenly, his eyes opened. The Shark was awake!

"Can't a super-villain have a little snooze?" he complained.

The Shark rushed at Green Lantern with his jaws chomping. Green Lantern put up a green shield, but the fishy felon bit down and broke it in two.

CHOMP! CHOMP!

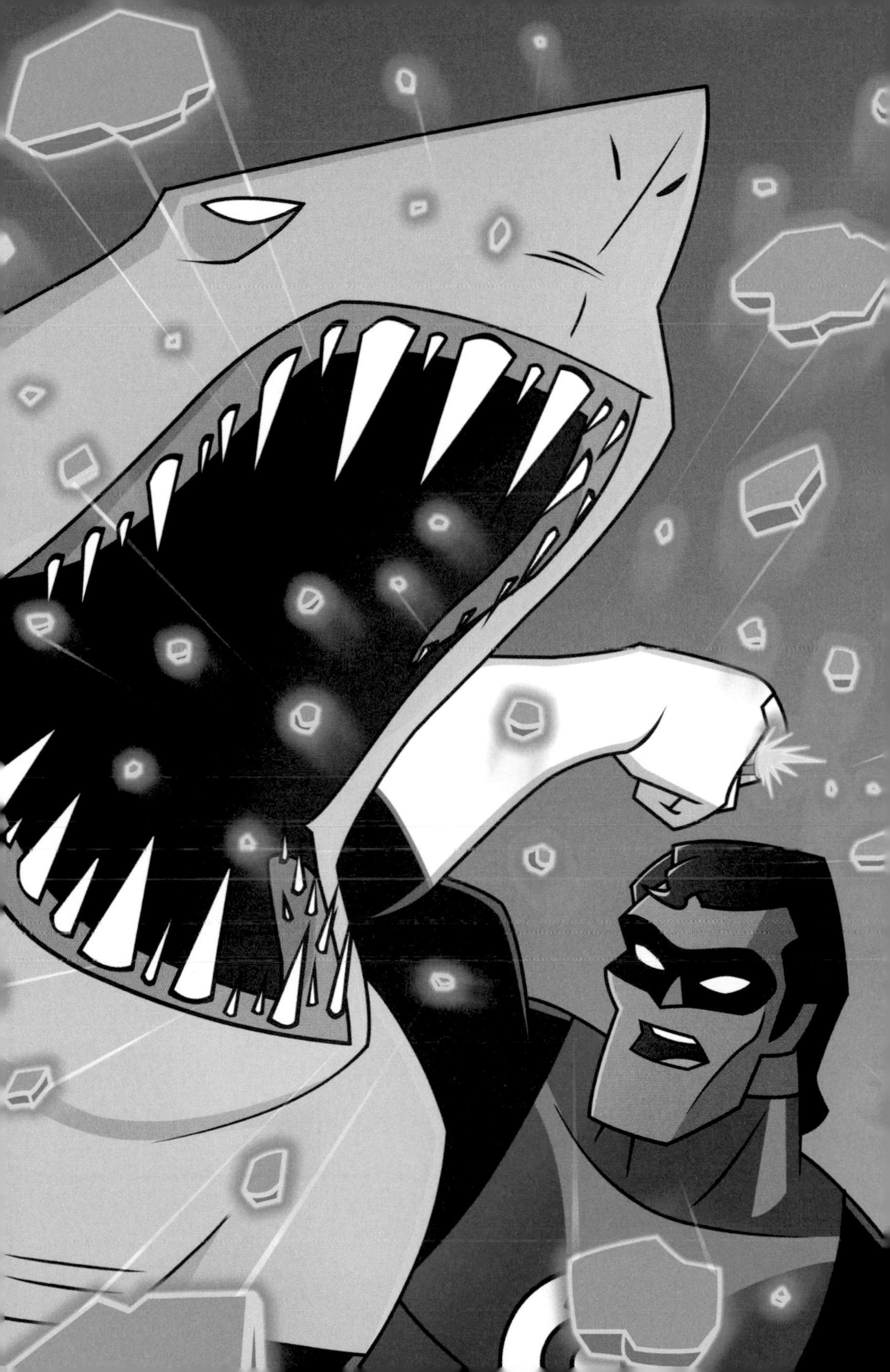

ZZZAPPPPPPP! Green Lantern fired an energy blast from his ring. The powerful shot hit the Shark and pushed him backward. For a moment, the water in the tiny cabin churned with bubbles, and Green Lantern lost sight of his foe.

CRRRREEEAAAK! The super hero heard metal being torn apart. Green Lantern could feel the Shark thrashing in the water. The force of the struggle knocked Green Lantern against a wall. Then the turbulence stopped. The water cleared.

Green Lantern saw a huge hole in the side of the ship. It had jagged teeth marks all around the edges. The Shark had chewed his way out of the shipwreck!

Green Lantern swam through the opening. He looked around for the Shark. The villain had not gotten far.

He was surrounded by hundreds of Green Lantern's fish creations. "Your finny friends can't stop me," the Shark declared.

"They don't have to," Green Lantern replied. "That's my job."

Green Lantern commanded his power ring to form tight chains around the Shark. The villain struggled to escape the restraints, but his arms and legs were pinned. He could not reach the chains to bite through them, either.

"Your reign is over," Green Lantern said.

The Shark did not reply. He hung his head and looked defeated.

Suddenly, a dark, gigantic shape came toward the super hero. It wriggled through the water like a snake. Green Lantern could not see exactly what it was at first.

The Shark looked up at the creation and smiled. "You make little green fish, Green Lantern," the villain said. "I make monsters!"

A giant sea serpent made of twisted kelp rushed through the water. It gulped down a mouthful of Green Lantern's fish army in its first pass. When it turned to come back, the rest of the fish scattered.

"See, even your ring creations fear my power," the Shark bragged.

"No," Green Lantern said. "If I'm not afraid of you, they're not afraid of you."

The swarm of green fish came back and attacked the seaweed serpent from all sides. They gnawed on the fronds that made up its body. Thousands of tiny teeth tore at the monster. MUNCH! MUNCH!

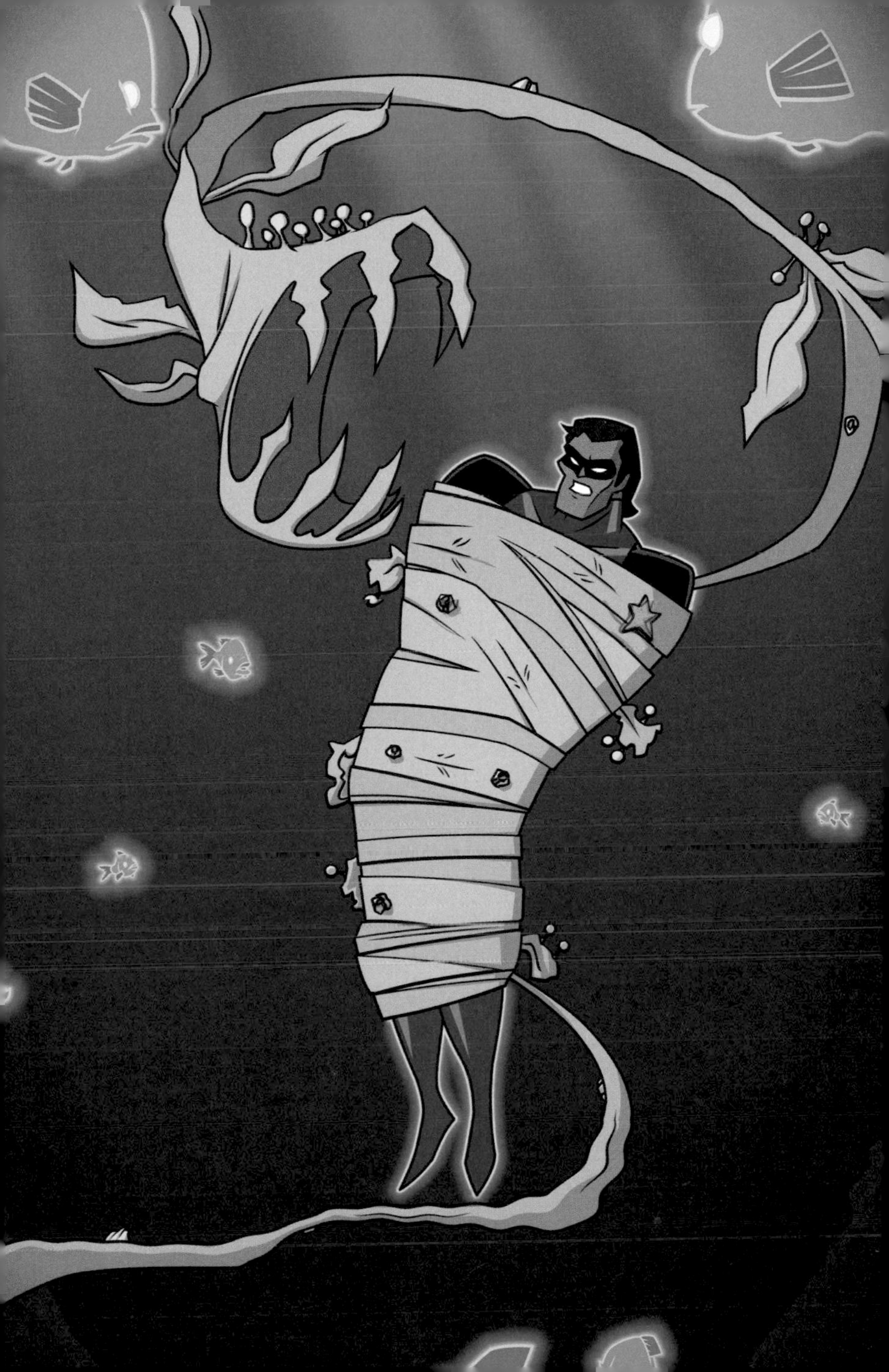

The serpent broke free from its attackers and rushed toward Green Lantern. The hero raised his power ring and pointed it at the monster. The serpent swerved at the last second. It wrapped its tail around the Shark and swam away with him. Green Lantern followed them, but it was hard to see in the murky water.

At last, Green Lantern saw a green glow in the distance. He swam toward it. He found the energy chains lying on the sea floor. The Shark had escaped and left them behind.

"The Shark is as slippery as an eel," Green Lantern said. "He keeps getting away from me, but not for long. I'm going to win this battle once and for all."

CHAPTER 5

FEEDING FRENZY

Green Lantern flew high into the sky, searching for signs of the Shark. He knew the villain would try to create more fear in the people of Coast City. The Shark was still hungry.

A cargo ship sailed toward the harbor, loaded with big metal containers stacked on its deck. Although the ship was extremely heavy, the vessel suddenly rose into the air! The water all around it moved in a giant circle like a whirlpool. It quickly formed into a massive waterspout.

"That looks like the Shark's handiwork," Green Lantern said.

Nearby, the Shark rested comfortably on a pillow of seawater. He didn't notice Green Lantern streaking through the sky toward him. He was too busy feasting on the fear.

Green Lantern commanded the power ring to form a huge clamshell. The shell closed over the Shark.

"That should hold you while I rescue the ship," Green Lantern said.

A giant fishing rod and hook formed above the cargo vessel. Green Lantern guided the hook to snag the ship's control tower. Then he reeled in the ship until it was lifted out of the waterspout. He placed the vessel in the calm waters of the harbor.

"Thanks, Green Lantern!" the crew captain said. "I never thought my ship would be the catch of the day!"

"I always practice catch and release," Green Lantern replied. "Except when it comes to super-villains."

The hero turned back to the clamshell holding the Shark. He was surprised to see a gaping hole in the bottom. The Shark had chomped through it!

He hadn't traveled far. The villain was still greedy for the taste of human fear. He wanted more! The Shark looked toward the shoreline for his next meal.

The beaches were crowded with people enjoying the beautiful day. Kids splashed in the water and played in the sand. Families were having picnics.

The lifeguards sat in their towers and watched over everyone's safety. They were the first to see the danger. A giant tidal wave was coming toward the beach!

The Shark rode on top of the wave. He controlled it with his powerful mind. The closer he got to the shore, the stronger he could taste the fear and panic. People were screaming and running. Children were crying.

"Their terror is delicious!" the Shark laughed. "More! More!"

The Shark made the wave even larger. Suddenly, Green Lantern was riding the wave next to the Shark. He was on a green surfboard.

"Surf's up," Green Lantern said. "Too bad you're going to have a wipeout."

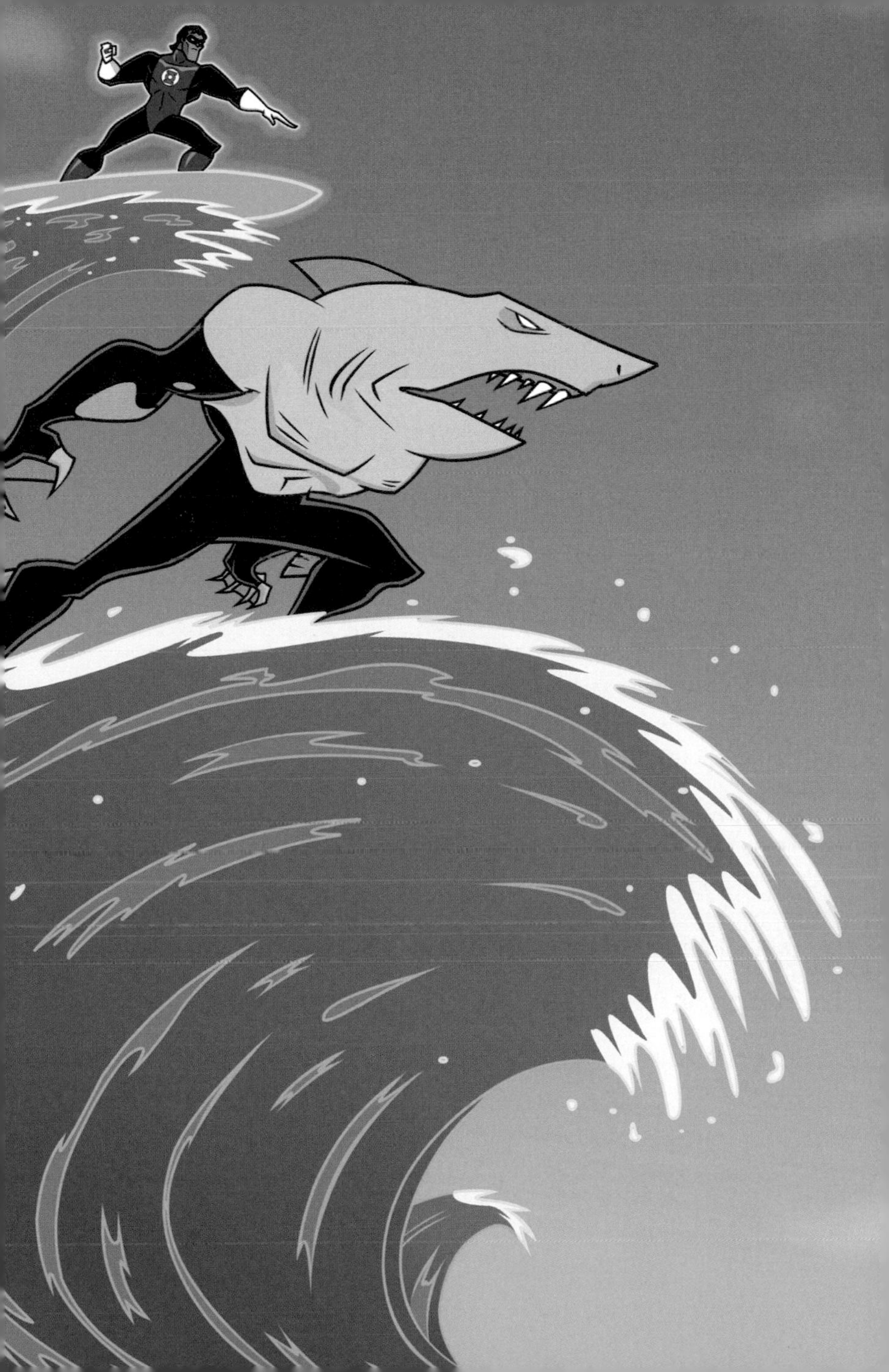

Green Lantern jumped off his surfboard and into the sky. He pointed his power ring toward the shore. A giant green seawall formed between the tidal wave and the beach. The barrier stretched along the whole shoreline. It was too late for the Shark to stop the tidal wave. It crashed against the seawall, and so did the Shark.

KRASSHH! The super-villain was knocked out.

"Excellent," Green Lantern said.

Green Lantern formed a green energy cage around the Shark and lifted him out of the water. The Shark was too groggy to resist. Then Green Lantern flew away from Coast City with his captive.

"I'm taking you where you can't use water as a weapon," Green Lantern said.

Soon, Green Lantern flew over the Mojave Desert. The land was as dry as an old bone. This is where he landed. Green Lantern created a giant aquarium with a roof to protect it from the sun. It even had a small shipwreck inside. This is where Green Lantern put the Shark.

"Welcome to your new home," Green Lantern said.

"This puny fishbowl won't hold me for long," the Shark promised.

"How far will you get in the desert?" Green Lantern said. "The fishbowl is the safest place for you."

The Shark looked around at the bleak landscape. There was nothing but hot sand for as far as he could see. The only water was in the tank. It was the perfect prison.

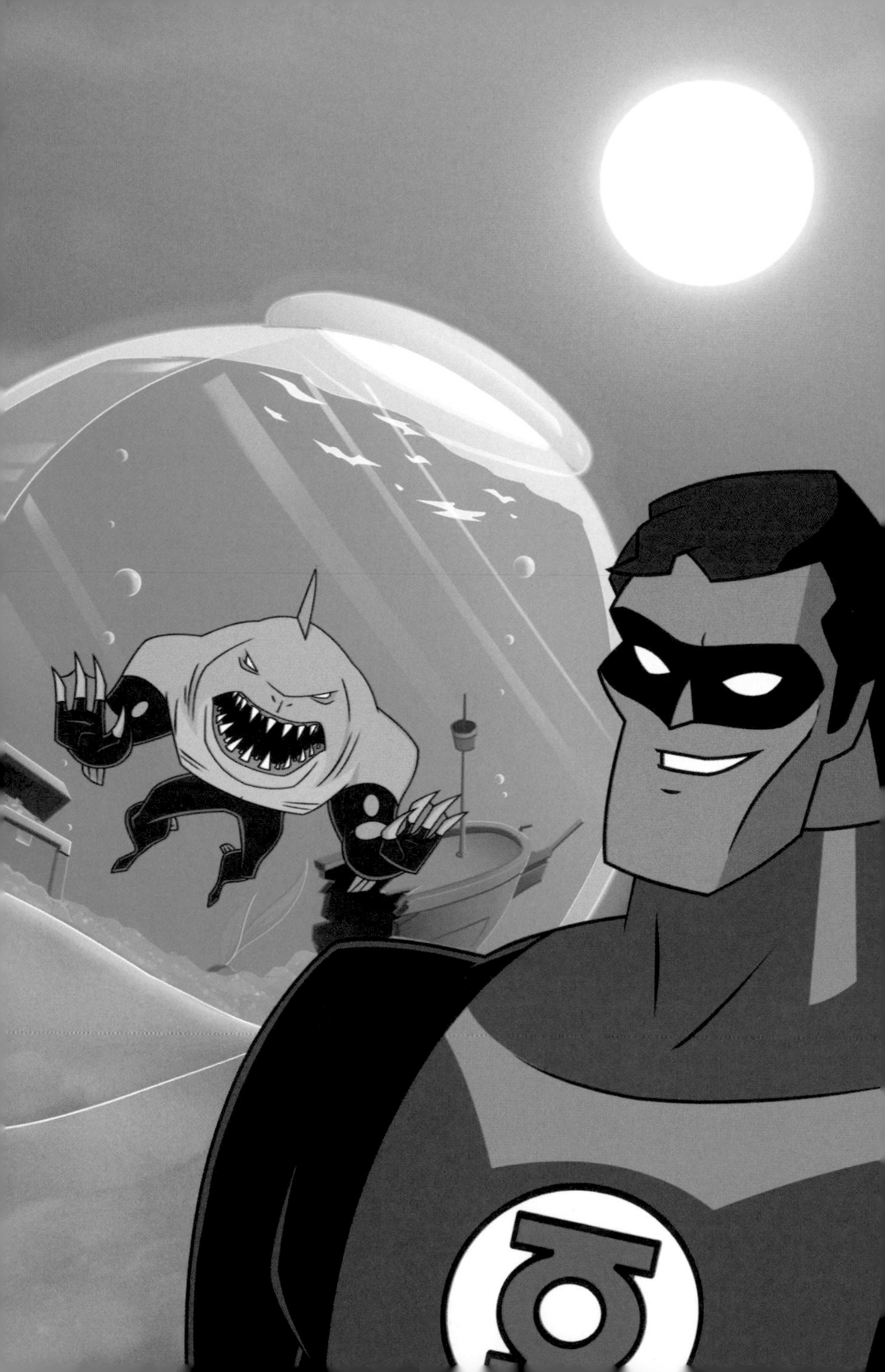

"I will have my revenge on you, Green Lantern!" the Shark threatened. He was still trying to fill his enemy with fear.

"Maybe someday," Green Lantern replied with a grin. "But right now, I have other fish to fry."

The super hero raised his power ring toward the blazing sun overhead. "In brightest day," Hal began. Then he soared toward the heavens, ready to take on evil's enduring might.

SHARK

REAL NAME: Karshon

OCCUPATION: Villain

HEIGHT: 6' 2" **WEIGHT:** 243 lbs.

EYES: Black **HAIR:** None

POWERS/ABILITIES: Ability to control objects and communicate using only his mind.

BIOGRAPHY

When radiation leaked from a nuclear power plant into the ocean, a regular tiger shark transformed into a vicious humanoid called the Shark. Although he's equipped with razor-sharp teeth, this beast prefers to feed on fear. With each horrified victim, the underwater marauder grows more and more powerful. Besides his enormous physique, the Shark's mental capacity is even more terrifying. The villain's ability to control objects and communicate with his mind make him a formidable foe to the World's Greatest Super Heroes, including Hal Jordan.

The super-villain Shark has all the abilities of a regular shark, including being able to dart through the ocean and breathe underwater.

The Shark has a mental ability called psychokinesis (sye-koe-kuh-NEE-suhss), which allows him to move and transform objects using only his powerful mind.

The Shark communicates with other creatures using only his mind. This ability is called telepathy (tuh-LEH-puh-thee),

Green Lantern Hal Jordan is completely without fear, which makes him one of the Shark's greatest enemies. It also makes him one of the villain's greatest challenges.

BIOGRAPHIES

Laurie S. Sutton has read comics since she was a kid. She grew up to become an editor for Marvel, DC Comics, Starblaze, and Tekno Comics. She has written *Adam Strange* for DC, *Star Trek: Voyager* for Marvel, plus *Star Trek: Deep Space Nine* and *Witch Hunter* for Malibu Comics. There are long boxes of comics in her closet where there should be clothing and shoes. Laurie has lived all over the world, and currently resides in Florida.

Dan Schoening was born in Victoria, B.C., Canada. From an early age, Dan has had a passion for animation and comic books. Currently, Dan does freelance work in the animation and game industry and spends a lot of time with his lovely little daughter, Paige.

GLOSSARY

banquet (BANG-kwit)—a luxurious feast

corps (KOR)—a group of people acting together

galaxy (GAL-uhk-see)—a very large group of stars and planets

kelp (KELP)—a large, edible seaweed

marauder (muh-RAH-duhr)—a person or animal that roams about, raiding and pillaging

menace (MEN-iss)—a threat or danger

morsel (MOR-suhl)—a small piece of food

mutated (MYOO-tay-tid)—changed or developed from an original form into a different form

oath (OHTH) —a serious, formal promise

sacred (SAY-krid)—very important or deserving great respect

sector (SEK-tur)—a part or division of space dedicated for each Green Lantern to protect

siesta (see-ESS-tuh)—the Spanish word for an afternoon rest or nap

DISCUSSION QUESTIONS

1. Do you think the Shark's punishment fit his crime? How else could Green Lantern have taught the evil fish a lesson?

2. The Shark is half fish and half man. If you could transform half of your body into another creature, which animal would you choose? Why?

3. This book contains ten illustrations. Which illustration was your favorite? Why?

WRITING PROMPTS

1. Hal Jordan created a perfect prison for the Shark, but nothing can hold this villain forever. Write a story about how the Shark could escape his fishbowl prison.

2. The Green Lantern ring can create anything the wearer imagines. If you had a ring, what would you imagine it to create? Write about your creation, and then draw a picture of it.

3. The Green Lanterns have a sacred oath that reminds them of their promise to protect the universe. Write an oath that encourages your own heroic behavior.

MORE NEW
GREEN LANTERN
ADVENTURES!

ESCAPE FROM THE ORANGE LANTERNS

PRISONER OF THE RING

RED LANTERNS' REVENGE

SAVAGE SANDS

WEB OF DOOM

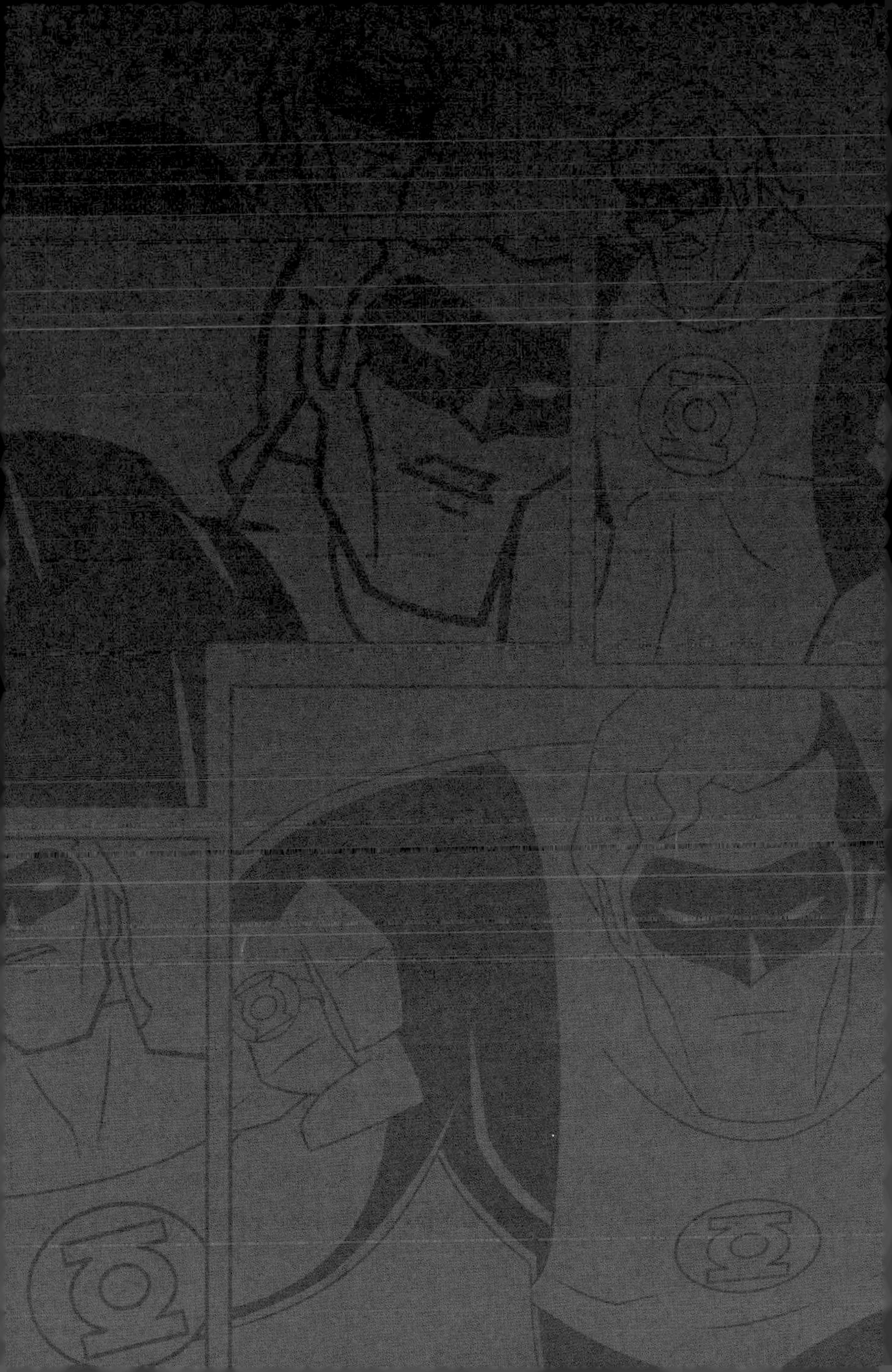

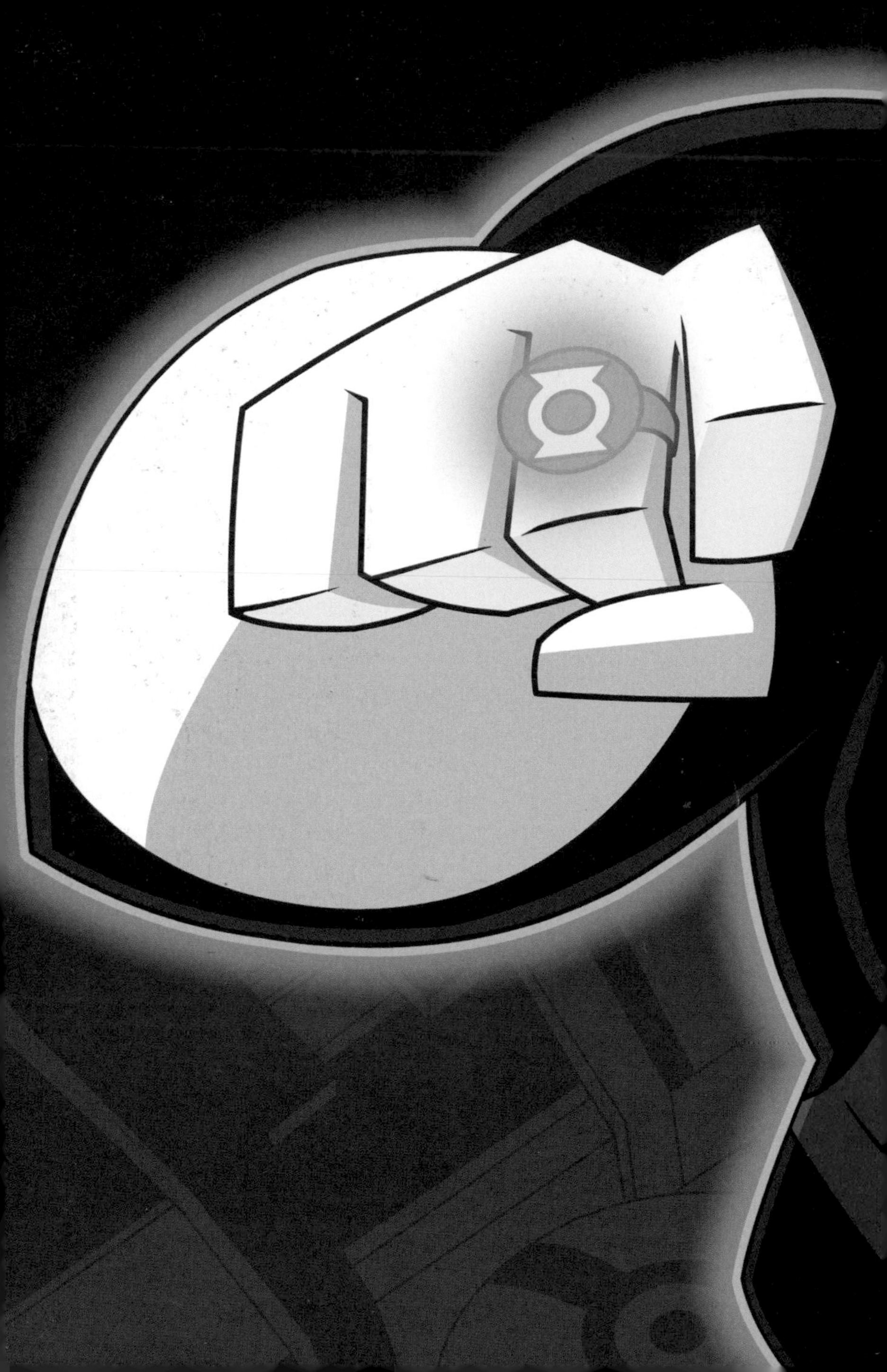